# Dawud Wharnsby

# A WHISPER of PEACE

*Illustrated by*

Shireen Adams

THE ISLAMIC FOUNDATION

# A WHISPER
## *of* PEACE

*First Published in 2014 by*
THE ISLAMIC FOUNDATION

*Distributed by*
KUBE PUBLISHING LTD
Tel +44 (01530) 249230, Fax +44 (01530) 249656
E-mail: info@kubepublishing.com
Website: www.kubepublishing.com

The songs on the accompanying digital CD were originally recorded with analogue equipment. Every attempt has been made to enhance and preserve, as closely as possible, the sound of the original recordings. Because of its high resolution, however, the CD may reveal some audio imperfections.

Book credits
*Author* Dawud Wharnsby
*Illustrator* Shireen Adams
*Book design* Nasir Cadir
*Editor* Yosef Smyth

Audio credits
*Qur'anic recitation* Jasser Auda
*Muazzin* Saleheddin Kanoun
*Additional voices* Feroz Bacchus, Tariq Bacchus *and* Maryam Wharnsby
*Remastering engineer* Chris Colvin, Studio A Audio Recording and Production, Kitchener, Ontario, Canada

The author would like to thank
Mohammad Husain Patel and family, Hamza Ouadfel, Khalil Musa, Akram Muhieddine and Ayesha Nawaz.

A Cataloguing-in-Publication Data record for this book is available from the British Library

ISBN 978-0-86037-534-0

Printed by Imak Ofset, Turkey

# ∽ C O N T E N T S ∾

# Bismillah

*Bismillahir Rahmanir Rahim, alhamdulillahir Rabbil ʻalamin.*
In the morning when we wake, *bismillah, bismillah,*
with every step we take, *bismillah, bismillah,*
with every word we say, *bismillah, bismillah,*
and every game we play, *bismillah, bismillah.*
*Bismillahir Rahmanir Rahim, alhamdulillahir Rabbil ʻalamin.*

With everything we do, *bismillah, bismillah,*
with everything that's new, *bismillah, bismillah,*
with every place we go, *bismillah, bismillah,*
and every friend we know, *bismillah, bismillah.*
*Bismillahir Rahmanir Rahim, alhamdulillahir Rabbil ʻalamin.*

*Bismillahir Rahmanir Rahim, alhamdulillahir Rabbil 'alamin.*
With every song we sing, *bismillah, bismillah,*
from every mountain, peace will ring, *bismillah, bismillah.*
*Bismillahir Rahmanir Rahim, alhamdulillahir Rabbil 'alamin.*

# Qad Qamatis Salah

Wake up from your sleeping, say "*Bismillah*" as you rise.
Wake up from your dreaming, make *wudu* and rub your eyes.
As the darkness turns into the dawn, pray *Fajr* to Allah.
As the moon cracks into daylight, sing "*Hayya 'alas salah*".
*Allahu akbar, Allahu ahad*
*La ilaha illallah, hayya 'alas salah.*

The burning sun begins to fall the second time we pray.
We turn our faces and our thoughts, the middle of the day.
Food, it keeps our bodies strong, a blessing from Allah.
*'Ibadah* feeds our spirit, sing *"Hayya 'alal falah"*.
*Allahu akbar, Allahu ahad*
*La ilaha illallah, hayya 'alal falah.*

Some of us, we race with time, we always lose the run,
for time is always keeping with the passing of the sun.
But we'll be straight upon our way if we bow to pray
throughout the day,
taking time for *'Asr* from our afternoon of play.
*Allahu akbar, Allahu ahad*
*La ilaha illallah, hayya 'alas salah.*
*Allahu akbar, Allahu ahad*
*La ilaha illallah, hayya 'alal falah.*
*Allahu akbar, Allahu ahad*
*La ilaha illallah, qad qamatis salah.*

As daytime drips away, the setting of the day,
we stand together side by side, at *Maghrib* time we bow to pray.
And when the sky is black, the moon awake so steep,
we pray the *'Isha* for Allah before we go to sleep.
*Allahu akbar, Allahu ahad*
*La ilaha illallah, hayya 'alas salah.*
*Allahu akbar, Allahu ahad*
*La ilaha illallah, hayya 'alal falah.*
*Allahu akbar, Allahu ahad*
*La ilaha illallah, qad qamatis salah.*

## Takbir (Days of Eid)

*Takbir! Allahu 'akbar!*

These are the days of `Eid, make *takbir* wherever you are.
These are the days of `Eid, *Allahu 'akbar.*
These are the days of `Eid, sing together everyone.
*La ilaha illallah wa lillah il-hamd.*

10

*Allahu 'akbar, Allahu 'akbar*
*La ilaha illallahu*
*Allahu 'akbar, Allahu 'akbar*
*Wa lillah il-hamd.*

Allah is great, Allah is great.
There is no god but Allah.
Allah is great, Allah is great,
and all praise to Him.
Allah is great, Allah is great.
There is no god but Allah.
Allah is great, Allah is great,
and all praise belongs to Allah.

# Al Khaliq

*La ilaha illallah.*
*Muhammadur rasulullah,*
*sallallahu 'alaihi was sallam*!

*Al Khaliq* made the oceans,
rivers, lakes, streams, and rain,
bow their waves in pure submission,
upon the earth to praise
His name.

*La ilaha illallah.*
*Muhammadur rasulullah,*
*sallallahu 'alaihi was sallam*!

There is no creature among us,
upon the air or in the sea,
that does not sing with wonder,
praising in community.

*La ilaha illallah.*
*Muhammadur rasulullah,*
*sallallahu 'alaihi*
*was sallam*!

The dry earth is a sign,
to all of mankind,
brought to life with peaceful rain,
and to us, Allah will do the same.

*La ilaha illallah.*
*Muhammadur rasulullah,*
*sallallahu 'alaihi was sallam*!

# Here We Come

Here we come, Allah!
Here we come to serve You!
Here we come, no partner do You have!
All praise to You!
The universe is Yours!
Here we come, Allah!
Here we come!

The world is a very, very big house,
many people, living in many rooms.
We must open all the doors up.
We must unlock them all today,
throw all the keys away.

Here we come, Allah!
Here we come to serve You!
Here we come, no partner do
You have!
All praise to You!
The universe is Yours!
Here we come, Allah!
Here we come!

Oceans and mountains divide us,
but the same fire burns inside us.
We must throw the world behind us.
With Allah is where you'll find us – here.
Here we come, oh, here!

Here we come, Allah!
Here we come to serve You!
Here we come, no partner do You have!
All praise to You!
The universe is Yours!
Here we come, Allah!
Here we come!

The world is a very, very big house,
many people, living in many rooms.
We must open all the doors up.
We must unlock them all today,
throw all the keys away.

Oceans and mountains divide us,
but the same fire burns inside us.
We must throw the world behind us.
With Allah is where you'll find us – here.
Here we come, oh, here!

Here we come, Allah!
Here we come to serve You!
Here we come, no partner do You have!
All praise to You!
The universe is Yours!
Here we come, Allah!
Here we come!

# Even Animals Love Qur'an

There was a chipmunk climbing up a tree,
I stopped to look at him and he stopped to look at me.
When I said "hello", he didn't understand and he went to run away,
I recited from Qur'an and he decided to stay.

Animals love to hear Qur'an, try it out some day,
they'll stop and listen carefully to every word you say.
Allah created animals, Allah created man,
and He sent a book to guide us all, even animals love Qur'an.

Sitting by a window to ponder at the sky,
I saw a little bird as it flew by.
I recited from Qur'an and it wasn't very long,
'til the bird sat near my window and it started to sing along.

Animals love to hear Qur'an, try it out some day,
they'll stop and listen carefully to every word you say.
Allah made the chipmunks and the birds, Allah created man,
and He sent a book to guide us all, even animals love Qur'an.

Playing in the yard on a warm, sunny day
a shy little kitten watched me play.
I bent down to pat him on the head but I think he was scared of me,
I recited from Qur'an, he smiled and brushed against my knee.

Animals love to hear Qur'an, try it out some day,
they'll stop and listen carefully to every word you say.
Allah made the chipmunks, birds and cats, Allah created man,
and He sent a book to guide us all, even animals love Qur'an.

Animals love to hear Qur'an, try it out some day,
they'll stop and listen carefully to every word you say.
Allah created animals, Allah created man,
and He sent a book to guide us all, even animals love Qur'an.

Animals love to hear Qur'an, try it out some day,
they'll stop and listen carefully to every word you say.
Allah created animals, Allah is *Ar Rahman*,
`cause He sent a book to guide us all,
even animals love Qur'an.

Allah made horses and dogs and bats,
and camels and gnats,
and pigs and cows and spiders and chickens,
and elephants and crocodiles and dolphins
and monkeys,
and beavers and sheep and lions and zebras
and whales and emus...

... "Hey, hey! What's an emu?"

Oh I don't know!
But He sent a book to guide us all,
even animals love Qur'an.

# The Prophet

Muhammad, *'alaihis salam*,
sat quietly in the evening.
His companion asked,
"Oh beautiful man, why do you sit here, grieving?"

"My *ummah*, those who follow me,
the future of their faith makes me worry 'til I cry.
My brothers and sisters in *islam*,
will they be strong and carry on after I die?"

The Prophet stood silently and prayed,
his beard becoming wet as he cried for all his fears.
"Oh Allah, don't let this nation fade!"
As he pleaded through the night,
the earth around him filled with tears.

"My *ummah*, those who follow me,
the future of their faith makes me worry 'til I cry.
My brothers and sisters in *islam*,
will they be strong and carry on after I die?"

As stillness fell over the land,
companions gathered near to where the Prophet lay.
As Ayesha, his wife, held tight to his hand,
the Prophet spoke again before he passed away.

"My *ummah*, those who follow me,
the future of their faith makes me worry 'til I cry.
My brothers and sisters in *islam*,
will they be strong and carry on after I die?"

"My *ummah*, those who follow me,
the future of their faith makes me worry 'til I cry.
My brothers and sisters in *islam*,
will they be strong and carry on after I die?"

Believers,
brothers and sisters in *islam*,
will we be strong and carry on until we die?

# Try A Little, Little Bit

If you try a little, little bit,
that's all that you can do,
when things get you up tight, bringing you down,
try a little bit to turn 'em around
and try a little, little bit,
that's the only thing that's best,
'cause if you set your mind,
you'll always find Allah will do the rest.

When Moses was in Egypt, running from the pharaoh,
he came up to the Red Sea and there was nowhere else to go.
He had to find a way across and he had to make it quick,
Allah inspired Moses, to hit the water with a stick.

Moses hit that water just as hard as he could hit,
and he stood back from that seaside
and he watched that water split!
Then Moses and his friends walked on through
to the other side.
They got away home free that day and all because they tried.

Yes, they tried a little, little bit,
that's all that you can do,
when things get you up tight, bringing you down,
try a little bit to turn `em around
and try a little, little bit,
that's the only thing that's best,
`cause if you set your mind,
you'll always find Allah will do the rest.

When Mary, the mother of Jesus was about to have her son,
she went out in the desert far away from everyone.
She was hot and tired and hungry from her *hijab* to her feet.
God guided her to shake a tree so she'd find food to eat.

Mary placed her hands on the palm tree with a slap and
a punch and a pound,
and suddenly ripe dates just started raining on the ground.

Yes, she tried a little, little bit,
that's all that you can do,
when things get you up tight, bringing you down,
try a little bit to turn `em around
and try a little, little bit,
that's the only thing that's best,
`cause if you set your mind,
you'll always find Allah will do the rest.

The Prophet Muhammad heard an angel call his name,
giving him God's message saying "Read and proclaim!"
Muhammad, he was shaken and he didn't think he knew
how to do just what that angel was asking him to do.

Muhammad learned those words and he taught them to
his friends,
now we have the Qur'an to guide us `til all time ends.

If you try a little, little bit,
that's all that you can do,
when things get you up tight, bringing you down,
try a little bit to turn `em around
and try a little, little bit,
that's the only thing that's best,
`cause if you set your mind,
you'll always find Allah will do the rest,
`cause if you set your mind,
you'll always find Allah will do the rest.

## A Whisper of Peace

A whisper of peace,
moving through the land,
Allah will surely run to us
if we hold out our hand.
A word of hope,
a call to every woman and man,
a light until the end of time,
this is *al islam*.

A smile of hope,
spreading to each face,
a charity – like moonlight –
guiding all our human race.
A universal song,
to pass on while we're keeping
pace.
A blessing without barrier,
and a gift of gentle grace.

# Glossary

*'Alaihis salam* – 'Upon him be peace.' (Arabic)

*Alhamdulillah* – 'All praise is to God.' (Arabic)

*Alhamdulillahir Rabbil 'alamin* – 'All praise is to God, Lord of the worlds.' (Arabic)

*Al Khaliq* – 'The Creator'. (Arabic) One of Allah's names.

*Allah* – 'God'. (Arabic)

*Allahu akbar* – 'God is the Greatest'. (Arabic)

*Allahu ahad* – 'God is One.'

*Ar Rahman* – 'The Compassionate'. One of Allah's names.

*'Asr* – A period of time which passes quickly. Also, *'Asr* prayer, the third time of worship in a day offered during the late afternoon.

*Bismillah* – 'In the name of God'. (Arabic)

*Bismillahir Rahmanir Rahim* – 'In the name of God, The Compassionate, The Merciful.' (Arabic)

*Fajr* – *Fajr* prayer, the first time of worship in a day offered before dawn.

*Hayya 'alas salah* – 'Come quickly to prayer'. (Arabic)

*Hayya 'alal falah* – 'Come quickly to success'. (Arabic)

*Hijab* – Something which veils. A garment worn by women of many faith traditions, covering their hair as an act of religious devotion.

*'Ibadah* – 'Worship'. (Arabic)

*Isha* – *Isha* prayer, the fith time of worship offered during the early hours of the night.

*Islam* – From the Arabic root letters *s-l-m* (*salam*) meaning peace. *Islam* is the act of entering into peace through wilful surrender or 'wilful submission' to God.

*La ilaha illallah* – 'There is no god but God'. (Arabic)

*Muhammadur rasulullah* – 'Muhammad is the messenger of God'. (Arabic)

*Maghrib* – Maghrib prayer, the fourth time of worship in a day offered during the moments after sunset.

*Muslim* – One who is engaged in acts of 'willful surrender' or 'willful submission' to God; the action of 'entering into peace'. The Arabic word '*muslim*' also stems from the root letters *s-l-m* (*salam*), meaning 'peace'.

*Qur'an* – '(The) Recitation' or 'That which is to be recited', in reference to the collected recitations of Muhammad, upon whom be peace, described within as being a revelation from God.

*Qad Qamatis Salah* – 'Come stand for prayer'. (Arabic)

*Sallallahu 'alaihi was sallam* 'Blessings upon him and peace'. (Arabic)

*Subhanallah* – 'Glory be to God.' (Arabic)

*Takbir* – A word referring to, or encouraging others to say, "*Allahu Akbar*", meaning 'God is The Greatest'

*Ummah* – A nation or community of people.

*Wa lillah il-hamd* – 'And for God is Praise'. (Arabic)

*Wudu* – The washing of certain parts of the body, as an act of worship. Often done prior to daily prayers.

## About the Author

Dawud Wharnsby was born in Canada in 1972. He has been writing stories, songs and poems for people of all ages for many years. When he is not travelling to sing with audiences around the world, he loves being with his family – growing vegetables, farming bees and fixing things that get broken around the house. Dawud loves adventures and being outdoors so much that he is an official Ambassador for Scouting (UK), encouraging young people to take care of the earth and build strong communities.  Dawud also serves as an Ambassador for the UK based charities MADE in Europe and Trees 4 Life.  The Wharnsby family lives seasonally between their homes in Pakistan, Canada and the United States.

Royalties from sales of *A Whisper of Peace* go to a trust fund supporting educational initiatives for children, directly overseen by the author.

Learn more about Dawud Wharnsby by visiting **www.wharnsby.com**

# Other children's books by Dawud Wharnsby